Crab woke up
and it was sunny.
That made him happy.
Happy, happy, happy!

2

Crabby Crab

by Liza Charlesworth

ISBN: 978-1-338-29785-0

Illustrated by Tammie Lyon
Copyright © 2018 by Liza Charlesworth
First printing, June 2018.

■SCHOLASTIC

"Make your bed," said his mom.
That made him crabby.
Crabby, crabby, crabby!

Crab built a sand castle.
That made him happy.
Happy, happy, happy!

A wave knocked it down.
That made him crabby.
Crabby, crabby, crabby!

Crab played soccer with his pal.
That made him happy.
Happy, happy, happy!

His pal scored a goal.
That made him crabby.
Crabby, crabby, crabby!

Crab got some ice cream.
That made him happy.
Happy, happy, happy!

The ice cream spilled on the sand.
That made him crabby.
Crabby, crabby, crabby!

Crab read a good book.
That made him happy.
Happy, happy, happy!

"Time for bed," said his mom.
That made him crabby.
Crabby, crabby, crabby!

"I am NOT tired," he said.

Crab got in bed.

Crab fell asleep.

Crab had a great dream.

Crab woke up
and it was sunny.
That made him happy.
Happy, happy, happy!